nickelodeon.

TEENAGE MUTANT NINJA TURTLES

Storybook
Collection

This edition published by Parragon Books Ltd in 2014

Parragon Books Ltd
Chartist House
15–17 Trim Street
Bath BA1 1HA, UK
www.parragon.com

ISBN 978-1-4723-5961-2

Printed in China

Storybook
Collection

PaRRagon

Bath • New York • Cologne • Melbourne • Delhi
Hong Kong • Shenzhen • Singapore • Amsterdam

CONTENTS

GREEN TEAM

Adapted by Christy Webster
Illustrated by Patrick Spaziante

A long time ago, a man named Hamato Yoshi bought four turtles at a pet shop. As he left, he passed a man on the street who was walking strangely, almost like a robot. Hamato decided to follow him.

In an alleyway, a rat ran up Hamato's leg. When Hamato shrieked, the strange man looked back and threw a canister at him – **SMASH!** The canister broke, splashing green goo all over Hamato, the turtles and the rat. The goo caused a chemical reaction! The turtles grew to human size and Hamato grew fur and a tail. He became a human rat!

That day, Hamato and the turtles became mutants.

Hamato Yoshi became Splinter. For 15 years, he raised the Turtles in the sewers below New York City. He was their *Sensei*, or teacher, but also a father-figure to the Turtles. He trained the mutant turtles in the ways of the ninja and they became the Teenage Mutant Ninja Turtles!

Over the years, the brothers had become strong ninjas, but they all had very different personalities.

Leonardo was brave and dedicated to his training. He liked to have a plan for every situation.

Michelangelo – the youngest of the four – was always joking around. He never missed an opportunity to prank his brothers!

Donatello was the brains of the bunch. He was never happier than when he was tinkering with computers and engines, or inventing a new machine.

And Raphael was the toughest Turtle. He loved to brawl - if there was a fight to be had, Raphael would be the first one to get involved!

On their 15th birthday, the Turtles wanted to see the city. The Turtles had never been above ground. But Splinter thought that people would be afraid of them.

"Do you think we're ready, Sensei?" Leo asked.

"Yes ... and no," Splinter replied. But in the end, Splinter relented and let them go to the surface. "Don't let anyone see you," he warned.

The Turtles cheered!

The Turtles peeked out of a manhole and saw the city streets for the very first time. It was dark and spooky and there was dirt and rubbish everywhere....

"It's so beautiful," Michelangelo said.

The city was filled with incredible surprises but, without doubt, the best one of all was pizza!

"I never thought I'd taste anything better than worms and algae," said Raph. "This is amazing!"

"It's great up here!" said Mikey.

As the Turtles headed back to the sewer, they saw a girl walking with her dad. Her name was April O'Neil.

"She's the most beautiful girl I've ever seen," whispered Donatello.

"She's the only girl you've ever seen!" Raph replied.

Suddenly, a large black van screeched to a stop. A group of strange-looking men jumped out and grabbed April and her dad!

The Turtles rushed to help but they were used to training as individuals, not as a team – they were terrible! They got in each other's way and kept bumping into one another. Leo hit Raph and Mikey tripped over Donnie.

While the Turtles were tangled up among themselves, the strangers escaped with April and her dad in the back of the van.

One bad guy was left behind and Michelangelo fought him one-on-one. Mikey unleashed his nunchuck fury and when his opponent fell to the ground, something strange happened. **BLOOP!** A weird pink blob popped out of the bad guy's chest – he was really a robot with a brain!

The brain scurried away before Michelangelo could show anyone. When he told his brothers about it, they didn't believe him.

Back in the sewer, the Turtles told Splinter about the failed rescue attempt.

"I need to train you as a team," Splinter said. "Next year you can go to the surface again."

But Donnie and Leo couldn't wait. They wanted to save April straight away!

Splinter nodded. "Then you will need a leader." He chose Leonardo.

The next night, the Turtles returned to the streets and tracked down the van that the bad guys had used to kidnap April and her dad. The Turtles hid in the shadows and waited for the driver to come back.

When he saw the driver coming, Leo whispered, "I have a daring plan."
But the other Turtles were already running towards the van!

The Turtles chased after the van as it drove away, jumping over rooftops
to keep up. Leonardo threw a ninja star and punctured a tyre! The van swerved
and crashed.

Raphael opened the back of the van. It was loaded with canisters of the same
green goo that had turned the Turtles into mutants all those years ago!

"This is huge," Leonardo said. "These bad guys have something to do with us."

"How is that possible?" Donatello asked.

"Anything is possible for alien robots!" Michelangelo said.

Raphael took a canister of goo from the van and shoved it in the driver's face.

"This stuff can turn you into a mutant like us," he said. "Tell us who you are and what's going on." He tipped the canister a bit, threatening to pour it over the driver.

"Okay! Okay!" the driver said, panicking. "My name is Snake. Those guys are called the Kraang. They're grabbing scientists. I don't know why."

Snake showed the Turtles the Kraang's hideout.

Raph wanted to attack right away, but Leo wanted to make a plan first. But while they were arguing, Snake escaped.

The Turtles chased Snake over the rooftops until they thought they had him cornered in a dark alleyway. But Snake had disappeared. Then Leonardo spotted him hiding behind some bins, but Snake didn't know they'd seen him.

Leonardo nudged Raphael – he had a plan. "Oh great, we let him get away," Leo said loudly so that Snake could hear him. "Let's take the van and drive it up to the Kraang's gate at midnight."

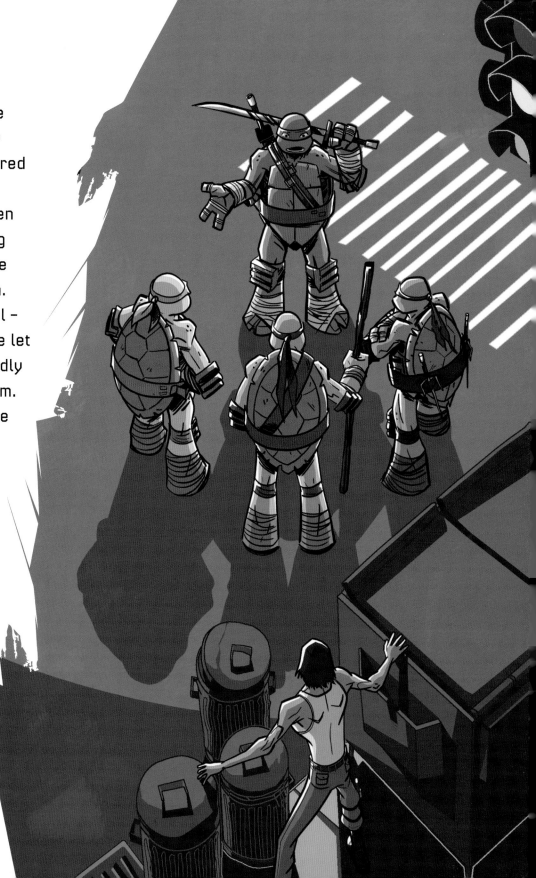

Later, the van raced up to the door of the Kraang's hideout. Snake and the Kraang thought it was the Turtles. **KABLAM!** They destroyed the van with their blasters! Green goo splashed everywhere and covered Snake ... but the van was empty. Where were the Turtles?

The Turtles had created the distraction so that they could sneak into the hideout. They discovered that the Kraang were really brain-like aliens that used robots to move around. The Kraang wanted April's dad, a famous scientist, to help them with an evil plan.

The Turtles searched the hideout for April and her dad and finally found them in a holding cell. Donatello tried to pick the lock but it wouldn't open.

Raphael started smashing the door instead. But just as he was about to break through, the Kraang returned and dragged April and her dad away.

The Turtles started to chase the Kraang, but Snake blocked their path. He wasn't just an ordinary gang-member any more, though – Snake was huge! He was covered in leaves and thorns. The green ooze had turned him into a mutant plant!

"It's Snake, but he's a giant weed!" Leonardo said.

"He's Snakeweed!" Michelangelo said. Mikey loved to name things!

The Turtles tried to fight their way past Snakeweed. But every time they sliced off one of his branches, it grew back in seconds.

"No fair!" Donnie shouted.

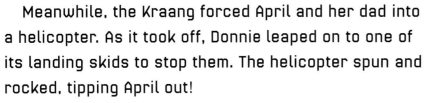

Meanwhile, the Kraang forced April and her dad into a helicopter. As it took off, Donnie leaped on to one of its landing skids to stop them. The helicopter spun and rocked, tipping April out!

Donatello caught her and jumped to the ground, but the Kraang flew away with her dad.

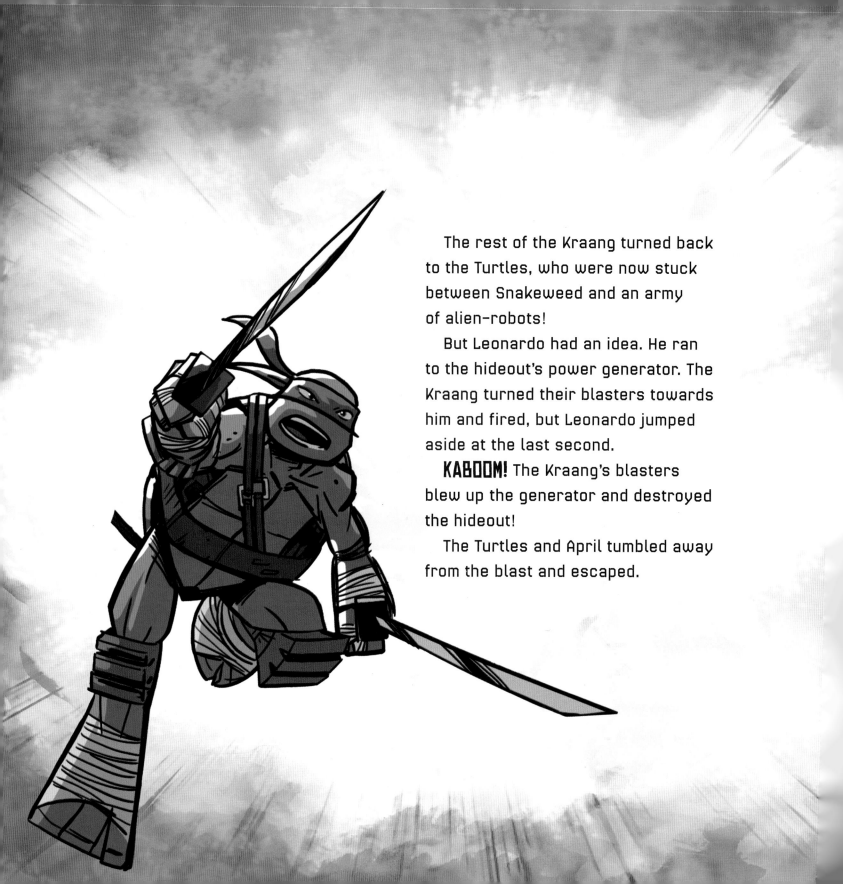

The rest of the Kraang turned back to the Turtles, who were now stuck between Snakeweed and an army of alien-robots!

But Leonardo had an idea. He ran to the hideout's power generator. The Kraang turned their blasters towards him and fired, but Leonardo jumped aside at the last second.

KABOOM! The Kraang's blasters blew up the generator and destroyed the hideout!

The Turtles and April tumbled away from the blast and escaped.

The Turtles accompanied April back home. She was safe but the Kraang still had her father.

"We won't rest until we find him," Donatello said.

"We?" asked April. "This isn't your fight."

"It is now," said Donnie. "Because we are a team!"

TEENAGE MUTANT NINJA TURTLES

DOUBLE TEAM!

Adapted by Christy Webster
Illustrated by Patrick Spaziante

Late one night, the Teenage Mutant Ninja Turtles were training in the lair.
Master Splinter led them in a practice drill.

"Are you fighting in slow motion?" Raphael teased Leonardo.

"I could go faster if I ignored my form, like you," Leo replied.

"Ignore this form!" With that, Raph attacked Leo and they continued sparring.

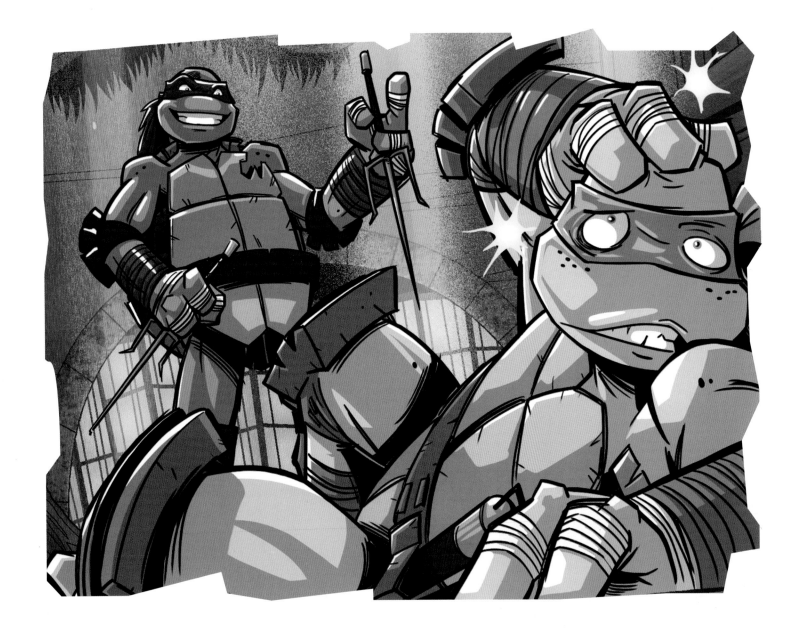

Before long Splinter intervened, stopping their fight. "You must learn to work together," he said. "Spar two-on-two against Donatello and Michelangelo."

"Is that fair?" asked Raphael. "We're way better."

Mikey scoffed. "At fighting, maybe."

"That's what I meant," Raph said.

Splinter signalled them to begin. As Raph said, he and Leo were the better fighters and they had Mikey and Donnie on the floor in seconds.

"You were right, Sensei," said Raphael. "Working together is fun!"

Training was over for the night, but defeat in the dojo had left Mikey and Donnie depressed.

"Look, guys," Leo said, trying to cheer them up. "Raph and I are better fighters, but you're still important to this team."

"You two think of us as some kind of B team," Mikey said.

Just then, the Turtles' friend, April, ran into the lair.

"What's wrong?" asked Donnie.

"Some guys from the Purple Dragons mugged me," April said. The Purple Dragons were a ruthless street gang. "They took my phone."

The Turtles were angry, but Splinter urged them not to rush into action. "Every fight is a risk," he reminded them, "you don't know where it will lead." But the brothers ignored his advice and headed straight to the surface to get April's phone back.

"We'll be careful," Leo promised as they ran out.

The Turtles found Fong, Sid and Tsoi, members of the Purple Dragons, in their hideout.

Raph and Leo gave the three of them a beating, easily shutting down their moves when they tried to fight back. Mikey and Donnie couldn't even get one hit in!

The Purple Dragons had a huge stash of stolen phones and gadgets hidden in their back room. "That looks like April's," said Donnie, collecting her distinctive red phone.

But before the Turtles could leave, the room started to shake. Dozens of tiny robots burst through a crack in the floor. Each one grabbed a piece of loot before disappearing back down the crack.

"Hey! They're stealing the stuff we stole!" Sid cried.

In the confusion, Fong grabbed April's phone from Donnie's hand and escaped out of the window.

"B team, get him!" Leo commanded.

Mikey and Donnie were offended but they went after Fong, leaping after him.

Raph taunted them as they left. "Don't be afraid to call for help!"

Raph and Leo smashed tiny robot after tiny robot, but many more escaped through the hole in the floor.

"Let's see where these things are coming from," Leo said, and the two Turtles jumped into the hole. Sid and Tsoi followed them, eager to see where their stolen loot was being taken.

Raph and Leo trailed the tiny robots to another building. Raph nodded at Leo, and they dropped through a skylight, landing in front of the robots' master.

"Dexter Spackman!" Raphael said. The Turtles had stopped this guy's evil plans once before!

"It's Baxter Stockman," Stockman corrected him. "And you can't stop me!"

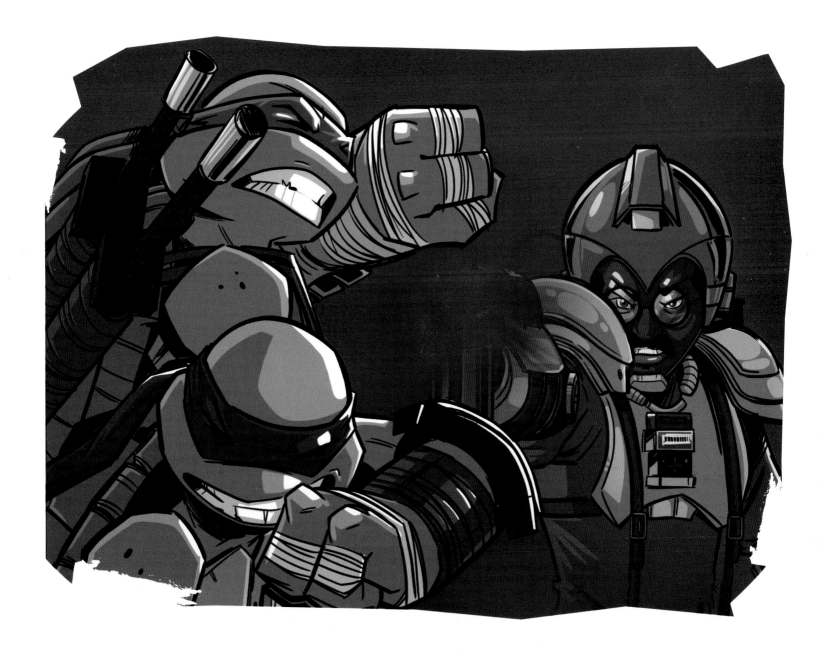

"These little robots are going to make me very rich," said Stockman. "I call them Mousers."

Just as the two Turtles were about to launch an attack, Baxter sprayed them with a red mist.

"Protect your eyes!" Leo shouted to Raph. The two Turtles coughed and sputtered but quickly realized they were fine. Just then, a horde of Mouser robots came rushing through the door towards them!

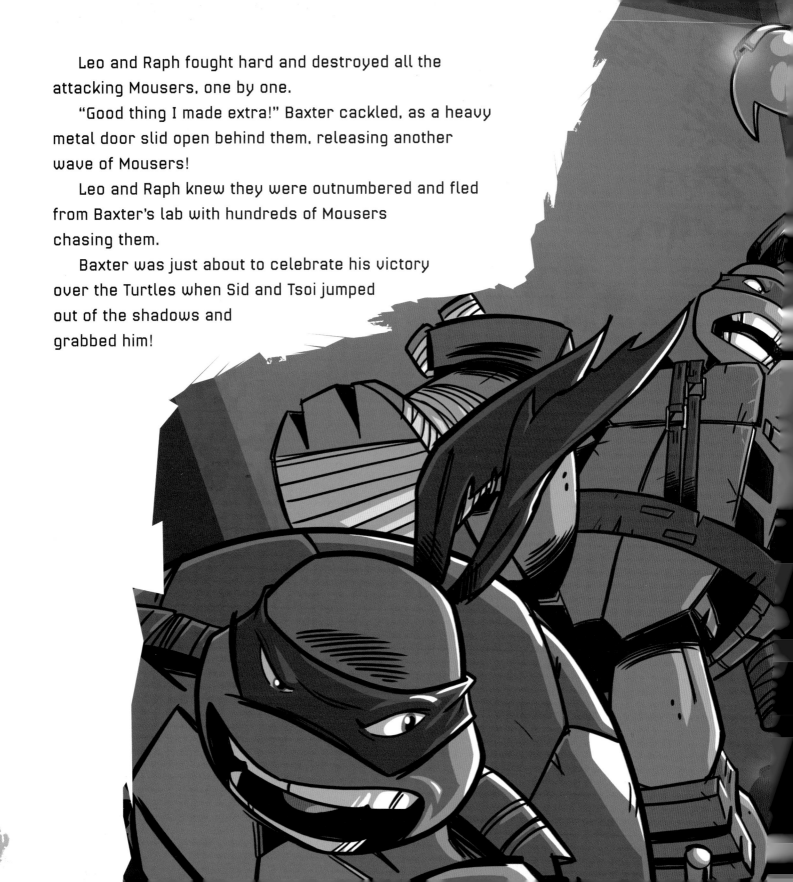

Leo and Raph fought hard and destroyed all the attacking Mousers, one by one.

"Good thing I made extra!" Baxter cackled, as a heavy metal door slid open behind them, releasing another wave of Mousers!

Leo and Raph knew they were outnumbered and fled from Baxter's lab with hundreds of Mousers chasing them.

Baxter was just about to celebrate his victory over the Turtles when Sid and Tsoi jumped out of the shadows and grabbed him!

Leonardo and Raphael ran all around the city, scaling rooftops and jumping alleyways ... but Baxter's Mousers kept up with them.

"It must be that stuff he sprayed on us," Raph said, leaping over a fence.

"Donnie would know what to do," Leo said. But after all the teasing he and Raph had dished out, they were too proud to call their brother for help.

The Mousers kept coming and Leo and Raph kept fighting back. "I've got an idea," Raph said finally.

The two Turtles pulled down a streetlamp and short-circuited the chasing army of Mousers. But just when Leo and Raph thought they could relax, another new team of Mousers rounded the corner and came after them!

"Okay, let's call Donnie," Raph said in defeat.

Meanwhile, Donatello and Michelangelo had followed Fong to a different hideout.
They watched through a skylight as Fong handed April's phone to Dogpound –
one of the Shredder's main henchmen!

"The Turtles want this phone." Fong told him.

Dogpound tapped the screen a few times. "It's locked."

Suddenly, Sid and Tsoi entered, dragging Baxter behind them as their prisoner.

Donnie needed to come up with a plan ... and fast!

Suddenly, Raph and Leo burst through a window.

"Not so fast!" Leo called.

"How did you escape my Mousers?" Baxter asked, confused.

"We didn't!" Raph said as Mousers started pouring through the shattered window behind them.

"This guy used robots to steal from us," Sid explained.

"I don't have time for this," Dogpound said. "I have to find the Turtles."

"Turtles!" Baxter cried. "I hate those guys. My Mousers are already destroying two of them."

Dogpound raised his giant paw and brought it down hard, slashing the ropes on Baxter's hands with his claw.

Dogpound handed Baxter the phone. "If you make robots, you must be good with electronics," he said. "Hack into this."

Suddenly, Raph and Leo burst through a window.

"Not so fast!" Leo called.

"How did you escape my Mousers?" Baxter asked, confused.

"We didn't!" Raph said as Mousers started pouring through the shattered window behind them.

With Dogpound distracted by the swarm of Mousers, Leo made a grab for April's phone and Raph freed Mikey and Donnie. The Purple Dragons had seen enough and simply ran away.

"We're here to save the day again," Raph teased.

"Looks like you were doing great," Donnie said, nodding at the Mousers.

But the battle wasn't over yet. The Turtles passed April's phone back and forth to keep it from Dogpound while trying to fend off the attacking Mousers.

"Baxter sprayed us with something," Leo told Donnie. "Now these things won't leave us alone."

Donnie picked up a smashed Mouser and looked at its insides. "A gamma camera!" he cried. "They must have sprayed you with radioisotopes. You can't get them off, but they will weaken with time. If someone else gets sprayed, though, the new signal will be stronger and attract all the Mousers."

Dogpound finally fought his way through the Mousers and charged at the Turtles. Leo and Raph took him on while Mikey and Donnie dealt with the Mousers.

"We need Baxter's spray!", Donnie shouted as he smashed yet another of the tiny robots.

"You mean that?" Mikey asked, pointing at Baxter.

Baxter stood next to Dogpound, aiming a huge spray-bottle at Leo and Raph.

TEENAGE MUTANT NINJA TURTLES

OOZE CONTROL!

Based on a teleplay by Jeremy Shipp
Illustrated by Nino Navarra

The Turtles had been training hard for a week so Splinter decided to give them a day off. Donatello was keen to use the free time in his lab, working on his latest creation.

"Are you still making that go-kart?" Michelangelo asked.

"It's an all-terrain patrol buggy," Donatello replied. "It has detachable sidecars and —"

SPLASH! Mikey flung a water balloon straight at Donnie.

"Dr Prankenstein strikes again!" he yelled.

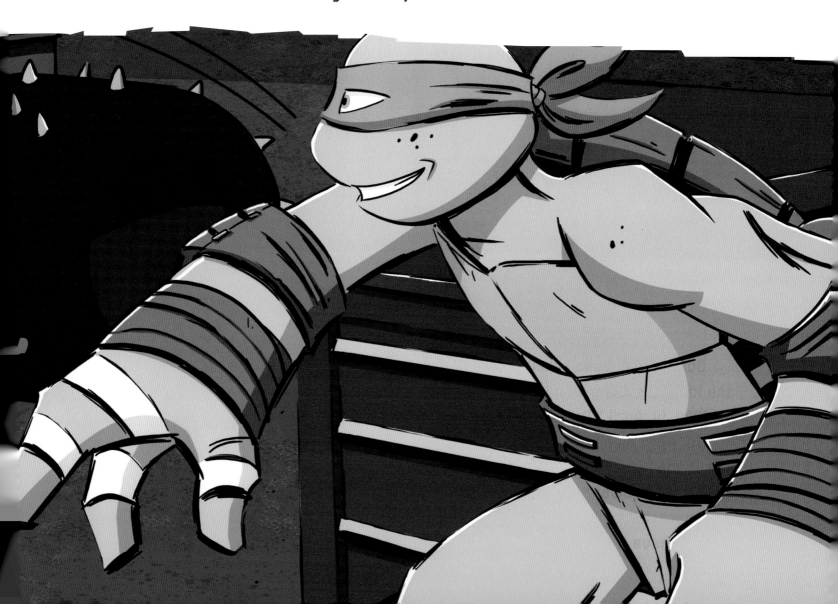

Donatello chased Mikey through the lair, but stopped as soon as he saw April in the lounge, talking with Leo.

"Um, hi, April," Donnie said.

But April didn't have time to chat. She had discovered something terrible. The leader of the Foot clan, an evil man known as Shredder, knew that the Turtles lived in the sewer. "He's going to destroy the entire sewer system to get you," she warned.

"We have to find out what his plan is," said Leonardo. "Let's go topside."

April led the Turtles to the warehouse where Shredder was hatching
his fiendish plot. She pretended to be a pizza-delivery girl to get inside.
"I don't like giving free pizza to the bad guys," whispered Mikey.
But the bad guys weren't fooled and they dragged April inside!
"We've got to save her!" shouted Donnie.

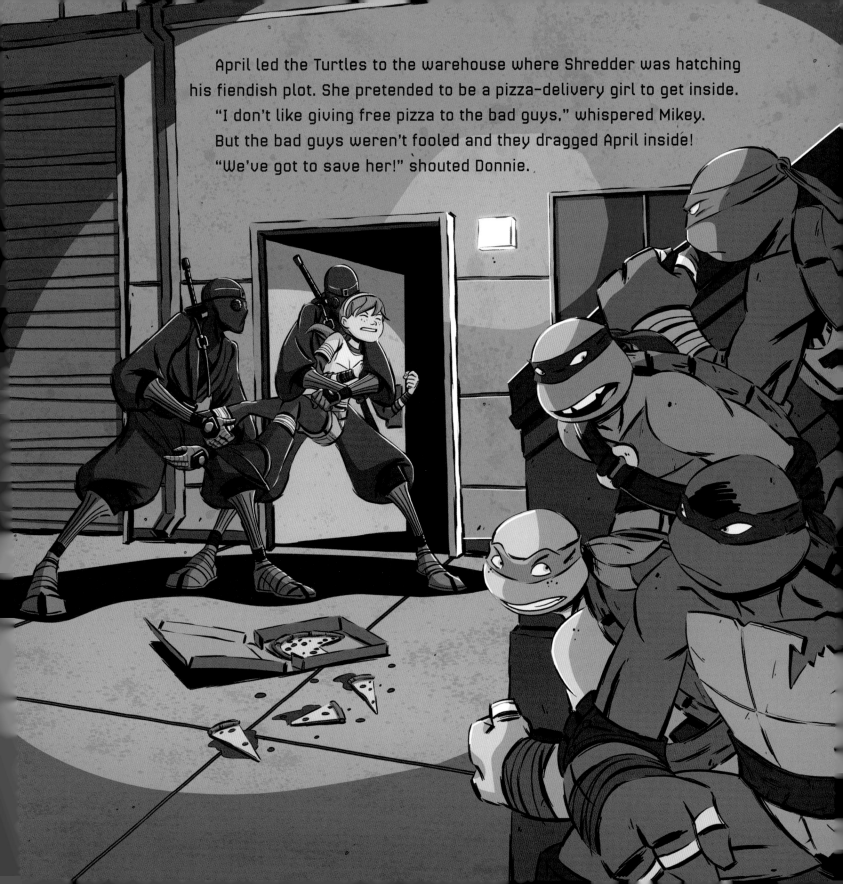

The Turtles crept into the warehouse and saw Shredder's ninja henchmen, the Foot Clan, filling a giant tanker truck with a strange chemical.

The brothers leaped right into battle, Leo swinging his shining katana swords and Raphael charging with his sai!

The huge truck roared to life and Michelangelo hurled a smoke bomb to stop it.

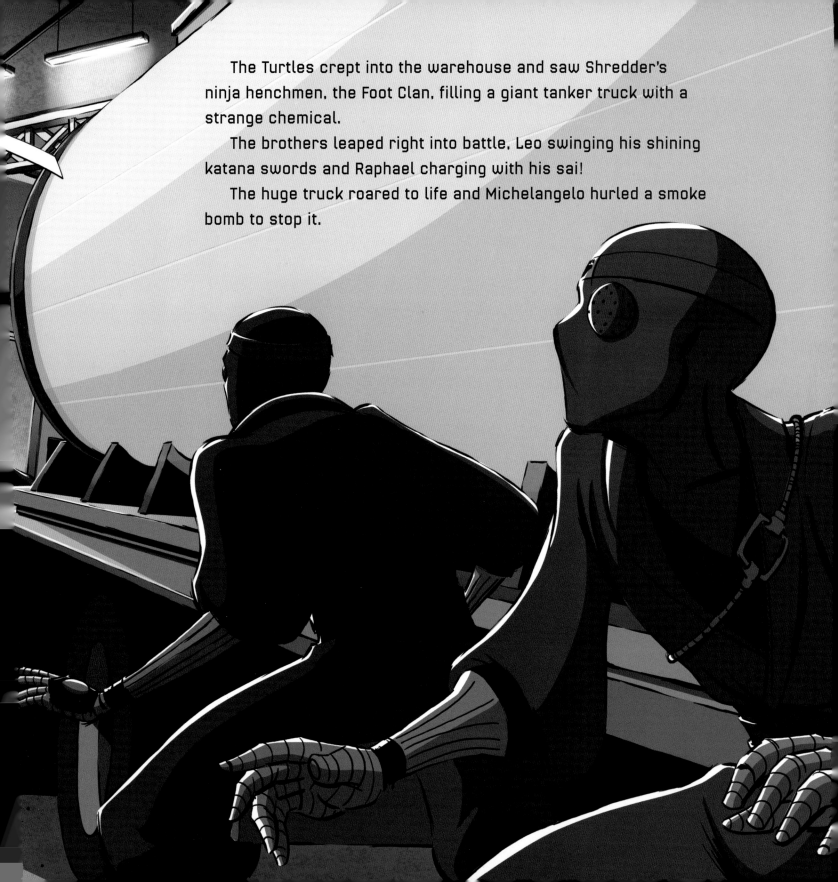

But the smoke bomb didn't work and the Foot Clan escaped. They bundled April into a white van, which thundered off into the night with the tanker.

"I've figured out Shredder's plan," Donnie exclaimed. "That tanker is carrying a dangerous chemical. When it comes into contact with water, it explodes. If it's poured into the sewer, everything will blow up – including the lair!"

"But we'll never be able to save April and stop the tanker on foot," said Raph.

"We're not going on foot," Donnie replied.

The Turtles ran back to the lair to get Donnie's new patrol buggy and zoomed back to the surface.

"Does this thing have a radio?" shouted Michelangelo, as they tore through the streets.

The Turtles' buggy skidded round a corner to find the tanker coming directly towards them!

Leo accelerated. "Watch this!" he said, pulling a lever.

The buggy split in half! Leo and Mikey swerved to one side of the tanker and Raphael and Donnie veered to the other.

"We'll go find April!" Raphael yelled.

"And we'll stop the tanker!" Leo shouted back.

Donnie and Raph tracked the van and Donnie hurled a ninja star at one of its tyres. The van screeched to a stop. The two Turtles made quick work of the Foot ninjas in a blaze of ninjutsu.

"Thanks, guys!" said April, emerging from the van.

A few blocks away, Mikey and Leo were about to attack the tanker, with Mikey wielding his nunchucks. The bad guys were dragging a hose from the tanker to an open manhole, ready to pump the explosive chemical into the sewers.

"We have to stop them!" Leo yelled. "Do you have any water balloons, Mikey?"

Michelangelo smiled. "I sure do!"

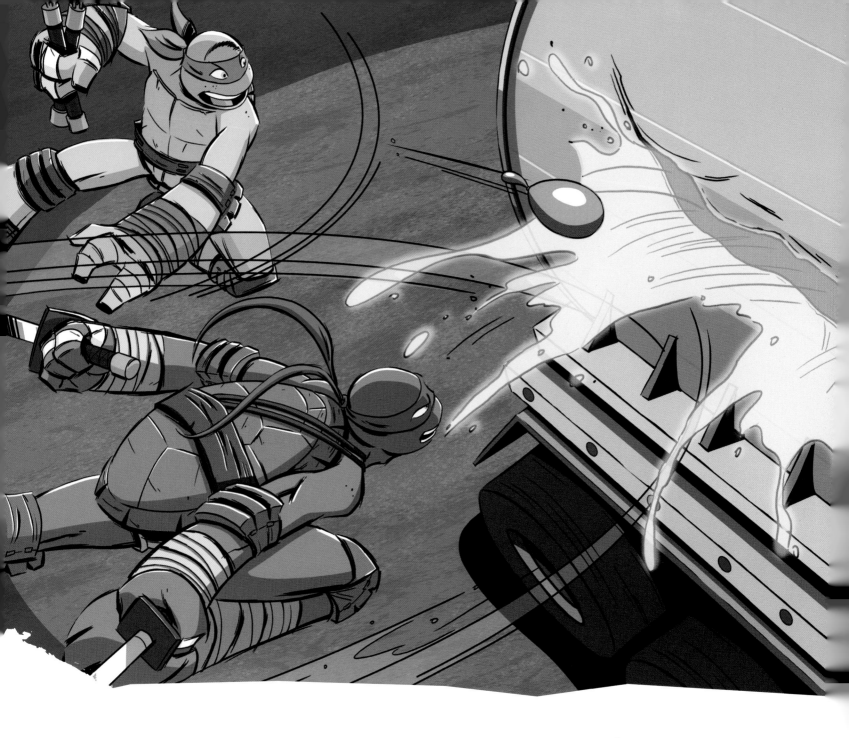

Leonardo leaped at the tanker and sliced it open with his swords.

Then Michelangelo hurled a water balloon at the chemical as it gushed out....

KABLAM!

The truck exploded as the two Turtles jumped to safety.

TEENAGE MUTANT NINJA TURTLES

ROBOT RAMPAGE

Adapted by Christy Webster
Illustrated by Patrick Spaziante

It was late at night and the Teenage Mutant Ninja Turtles were in an abandoned warehouse, battling their enemies, the Kraang!

The Kraang were blobby, weird-looking pink brains – and they used robots called Kraang-droids to carry them around and fight their battles.

SMASH! Raphael knocked out a Kraang-droid and a pink Kraang jumped out of it and scurried away.

THUNNNG! Donatello tried to use his wooden bo staff against another robot, but it bounced off! The robot wasn't damaged. "Are you kidding me?" cried Donatello.

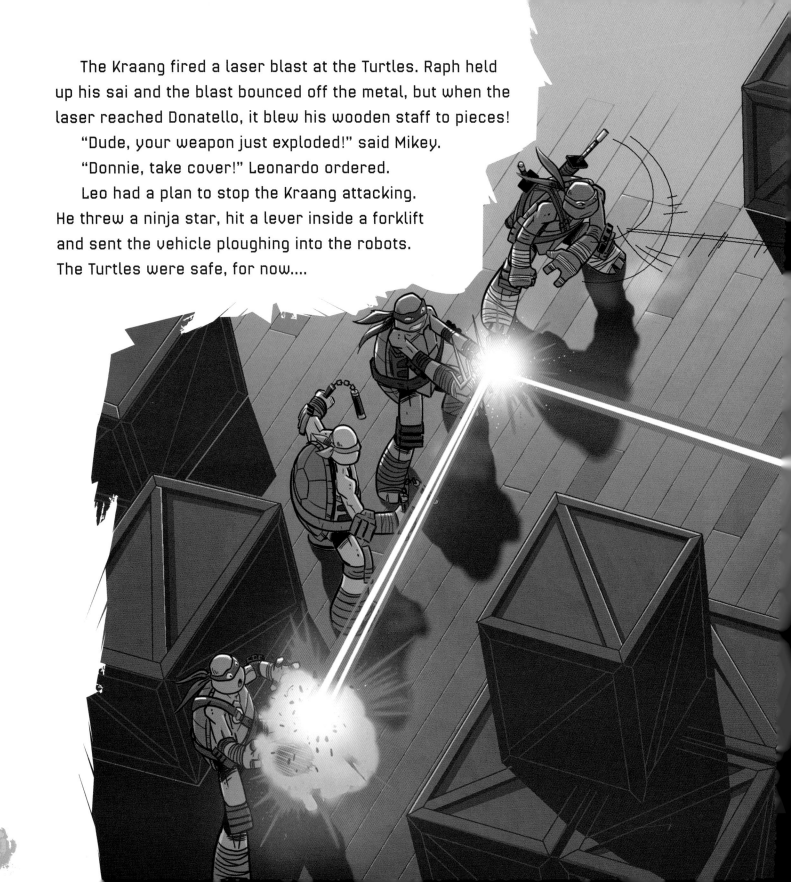

The Kraang fired a laser blast at the Turtles. Raph held
up his sai and the blast bounced off the metal, but when the
laser reached Donatello, it blew his wooden staff to pieces!

"Dude, your weapon just exploded!" said Mikey.

"Donnie, take cover!" Leonardo ordered.

Leo had a plan to stop the Kraang attacking.
He threw a ninja star, hit a lever inside a forklift
and sent the vehicle ploughing into the robots.
The Turtles were safe, for now....

At the end of the battle Donatello recovered an empty Kraang robot.

"Hey, guys, give me a hand with this," he said.

"What do you want that thing for?!" Raphael asked.

"Don't you want to understand how these things work?" Donnie was fascinated by the advanced technologies of the Kraang, so the Turtles helped him carry the robot back to the lair.

When they arrived, Splinter gave Donatello a new wooden staff.

"I can't keep fighting with this," Donatello told Splinter.

"You may upgrade your weapon," Splinter said. "But, remember, combat is not a video game."

"*Hmmm, 'video game'* ..." thought Donnie, "... *that gives me an idea....*"

The next day, the Turtles' friend April told them about a website she had made, where people could post messages. Someone had uploaded a video about a gas explosion in the warehouse district. April pressed pause. They could see a Kraang-droid in the background!

"We'll check it out tonight," Leonardo said. "We can't go in the daytime." Splinter didn't want people to see the Turtles.

"Well, I can," April said, and she went to investigate.

It was now dark outside, so Mikey, Raph and Leo went out into the city. They leaped across rooftops and waited on a ledge.

CLANG! CLANG! CLANG! Metalhead slowly caught up with them. Donatello was back in the lair, controlling the robot like a video game.

"It can do all the dangerous stuff while we stay safe," said Donatello.

"So it's for wimps," Raphael replied.

"Try it," Donatello said. "Attack it."

Raph, Leo and Mikey all attacked, but they couldn't even make a dent.

"Let's call it Metalhead!" said Mikey.

It was now dark outside, so Mikey, Raph and Leo went out into the city. They leaped across rooftops and waited on a ledge.

CLANG! CLANG! CLANG! Metalhead slowly caught up with them. Donatello was back in the lair, controlling the robot like a video game.

April met the Turtles on her way back from the warehouse district.

"We have to do something," she said. "The Kraang are going to poison the city's water supply with mutagen!"

She quickly led the Turtles and Metalhead back to where she had come from.

Outside the warehouse, April and Metalhead waited behind while Leo, Mikey and Raph sneaked up on the Kraang.

The three Turtles lurked in the dark, watching the Kraang-droids load mutagen onto trucks.

Leo decided he had seen enough. On his command, the three Turtles charged into the warehouse.

"HIIIII-YAH!" Raphael screamed, as they launched an attack.

Meanwhile, April and Metalhead saw an energy blast shoot through the roof
of the warehouse! They heard Michelangelo shout:

"THEY'RE EVERYWHERE! RUN! RUN!"

It sounded like the three Turtles had been cornered by the Kraang.

Donnie, who was watching the action through Metalhead's eyes, knew he had
to help!

Inside the warehouse, Metalhead suddenly came crashing down through the roof. The Turtles and the Kraang all stopped fighting and stared.

"Why are you standing like that?" Leonardo asked. Metalhead's arms were in a weird position.

"Don't I look heroic?" Metalhead said in Donatello's voice.

"No!" Leonardo shouted.

"Sorry," Metalhead said. "Wrong button!"

The battle continued. Metalhead really did seem invincible! Donatello watched from the lair, excited. He made Metalhead move faster and faster, blasting lasers all over the place. Finally, he found his target.

BOOM! The Kraang's pile of mutagen exploded.

The city's water supply was safe, but Metalhead had been damaged in the explosion.

Donatello lost contact with the robot. "Guys, if you can hear me, **RUN!**" he shouted.

Suddenly, a Kraang brain jumped out of its damaged droid body and on to Metalhead. Metalhead's eyes glowed red. Now the Kraang was controlling him! Evil Metalhead attacked the Turtles.

Donatello grabbed his bo staff and ran straight to the warehouse. He took on Evil Metalhead while the other Turtles fought the Kraang. Donnie dodged attack after attack from his own robot, until one powerful blast shattered his staff.

"Not again!" Donnie cried.

But then he spotted a loose beam on the ceiling above him....

"Come and get me!" Donnie called out to Evil Metalhead, tempting the powerful robot to take him on.

Evil Metalhead aimed another laser blast right at Donnie. At the last second, Donnie jumped aside and the laser blast struck the loose beam. As the beam came crashing down, it fell on to Metalhead!

Gears crunched and sparks crackled – the robot was badly damaged. Then Donnie followed up, using his broken staff to finish off Evil Metalhead.

Evil Metalhead was defeated! The Kraang brain jumped out of the robot and scurried away.

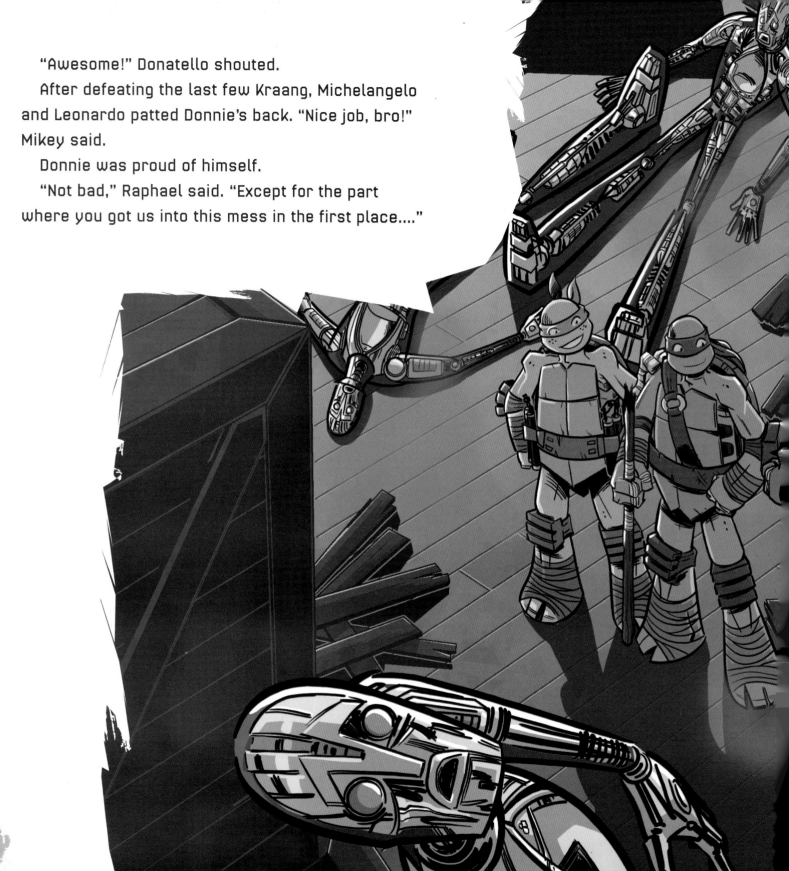

"Awesome!" Donatello shouted.

After defeating the last few Kraang, Michelangelo and Leonardo patted Donnie's back. "Nice job, bro!" Mikey said.

Donnie was proud of himself.

"Not bad," Raphael said. "Except for the part where you got us into this mess in the first place...."

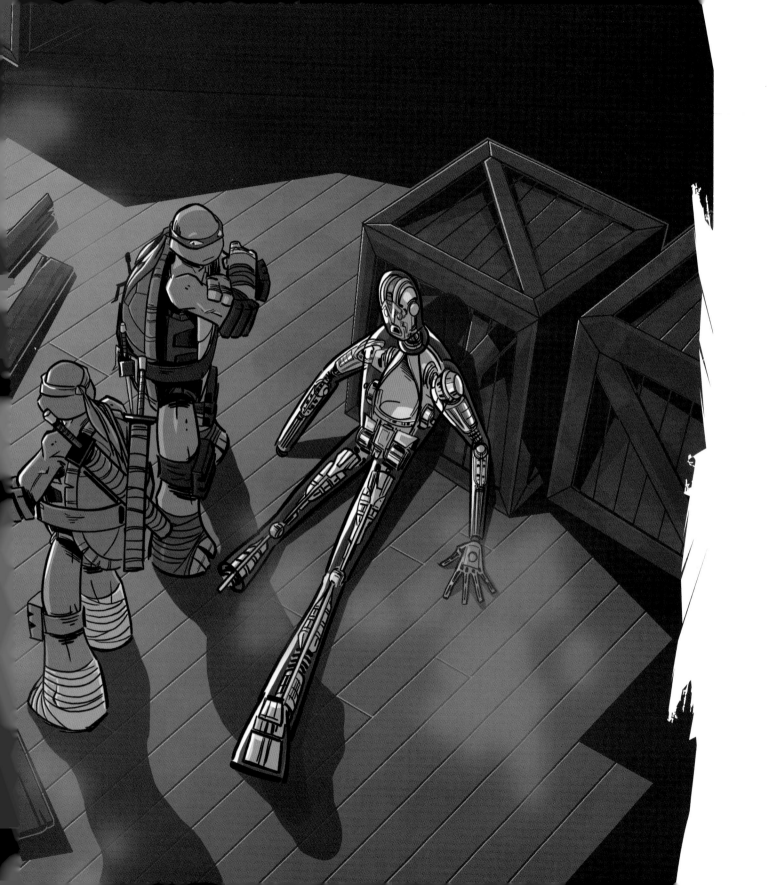

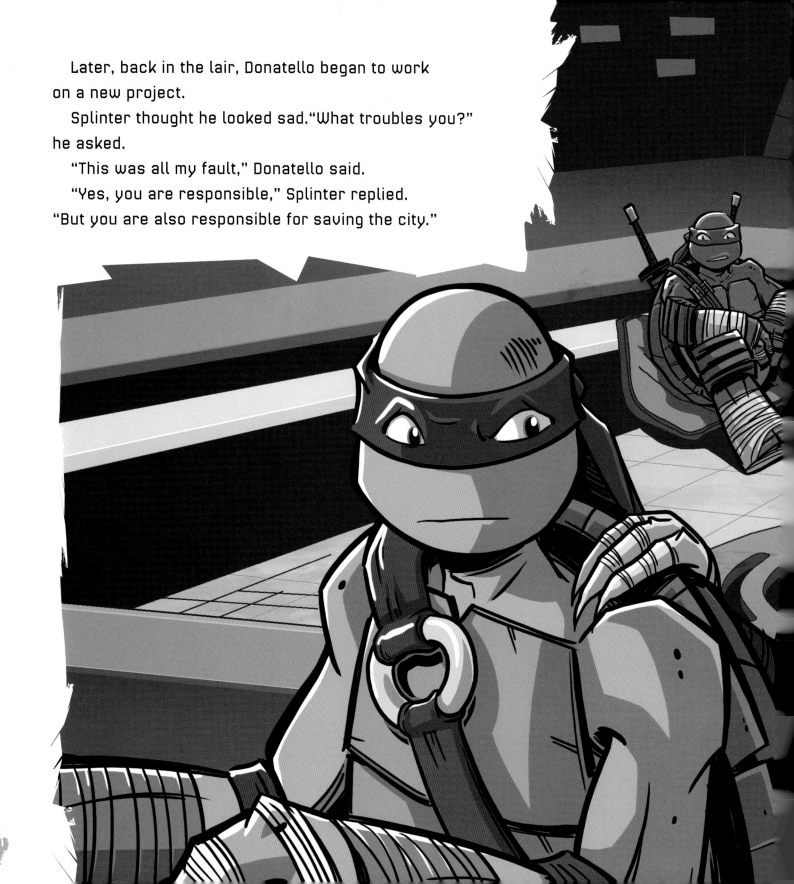

Later, back in the lair, Donatello began to work
on a new project.

Splinter thought he looked sad. "What troubles you?"
he asked.

"This was all my fault," Donatello said.

"Yes, you are responsible," Splinter replied.
"But you are also responsible for saving the city."

Splinter's words helped Donatello to feel better.
"In the end," he said, "there was nothing better than
a wooden stick ... "

" ... except a laser-guided wooden stick!"

Donatello held up the new weapon he was working on - a bo staff with a laser!

But then he slammed the new bo staff on the ground and it started to make a strange sound....

"It's not supposed to do that!" Donatello cried. **"RUN!"**

nickelodeon™
TEENAGE MUTANT NINJA TURTLES™
MONKEY BUSINESS

Based on a teleplay by Ron Corcillo and Russ Carney
Illustrated by Patrick Spaziante

One day, while training in the dojo, Donatello and Michelangelo began arguing about the best methods of defence.

"Mikey, you need a plan for every attack," said Donatello. "Isn't that right, Splinter?"

"You must be fully in the moment so you can fight without thinking," replied Splinter.

Just then, the Turtles' friend April O'Neil ran into the dojo.

"According to the news, a scientist named Tyler Rockwell is missing," she said. April's father, an important scientist, had been captured by an alien race called the Kraang. "Maybe the Kraang have taken this guy, too."

Donatello and April decided to investigate. They raced to Dr Rockwell's abandoned lab. While searching the dark room, Donatello found a canister of mutagen – the mysterious Kraang chemical that had mutated the Turtles. Suddenly, out of nowhere, a shadowy figure attacked!

Donatello overcame the attacker. His name was Dr Falco. He was the missing doctor's assistant. He revealed that Dr Rockwell had been using the mutagen to perform strange experiments on a monkey.

"It looks like the monkey didn't like being locked up," Donatello said, spotting a mangled cage. He noticed a computer flash drive and slyly took it.

As Donatello and April left the lab, a giant monkey leaped from above!
"Watch out!" April yelled. "He's a dangerous mutant!"
"That makes two of us!" Donatello replied.
Donnie charged, swinging his bo staff, but the raging monkey was incredibly strong and knocked him back easily.

The monkey locked April in his massive arms, then paused.
They had a connection. April realized she could read the monkey's mind and he could read hers. "Everything's okay," she whispered reassuringly. The monkey seemed to relax, but then ran away.

Back at the lair, Donatello analysed the flash drive and learned that Dr Rockwell was using the mutagen to give his lab animals psychic powers.

"That monkey can read minds!" Donatello exclaimed.

"Cool," Michelangelo said. "I wonder if he could tell me what I'm thinking – I've always wanted to know."

April and the Turtles went to find the monkey.

The Turtles traced the monkey to a dark alley. They couldn't match his strength and speed – until Mikey rolled up on his skateboard swinging a rope. Mikey lassoed him!
April stared at the monkey, who stared back at her. "He only reacts violently to angry thoughts," she said calmly.

"Great. We got the monkey, but we're not any closer to finding Dr Rockwell," said Raphael.

An idea suddenly occurred to April. She turned to the Turtles, "I think this is Dr Rockwell!"

The Turtles returned the monkey to the lab, where they made another startling discovery: Dr Falco had used the mutagen on Dr Rockwell!

"He was my guinea pig," Dr Falco confessed.

"Well, it didn't work," Michelangelo said. "You turned him into a monkey!"

His katana swords flashing, Leonardo sprang at Dr Falco.

The Turtles quickly realized that Dr Falco had used the mutagen on himself, too – he could read the Turtles' minds! Knowing their attack plans before they struck, Dr Falco was more than a match for the Turtles.

Suddenly, Donatello remembered Splinter's words: "You must be fully in the moment so you can fight without thinking."

He cleared his mind and launched himself like a bolt of lightning. His flying kick hurled Dr Falco across the room.

Dr Falco realized he was defeated and ran away.

The Turtles knew they couldn't leave Dr Rockwell tied up, so they released him and he bounded out of a window.

They immediately heard a woman scream and a car crash.

"Um, maybe New York City isn't the best place for a psychic monkey who reacts to angry thoughts," said Raphael.

nickelodeon™
TEENAGE MUTANT NINJA TURTLES™

MIKEY'S MONSTER

Adapted by Hollis James
Illustrated by Patrick Spaziante

In the Kraang's secret hideout, a giant creature was on the loose. In their robotic Kraang-droid bodies, a team of Kraang chased after the beast, firing their laser blasters.

BLAM! BLAM! A blast hit the creature as it tried to escape and it collapsed on the floor.

The Kraang-droids gathered around the fallen creature, which looked like a giant alligator. One of its enormous clawed hands clung tightly to a glowing object.

"Give to Kraang the power cell that Kraang demands that you give to Kraang!" said the head Kraang-droid.

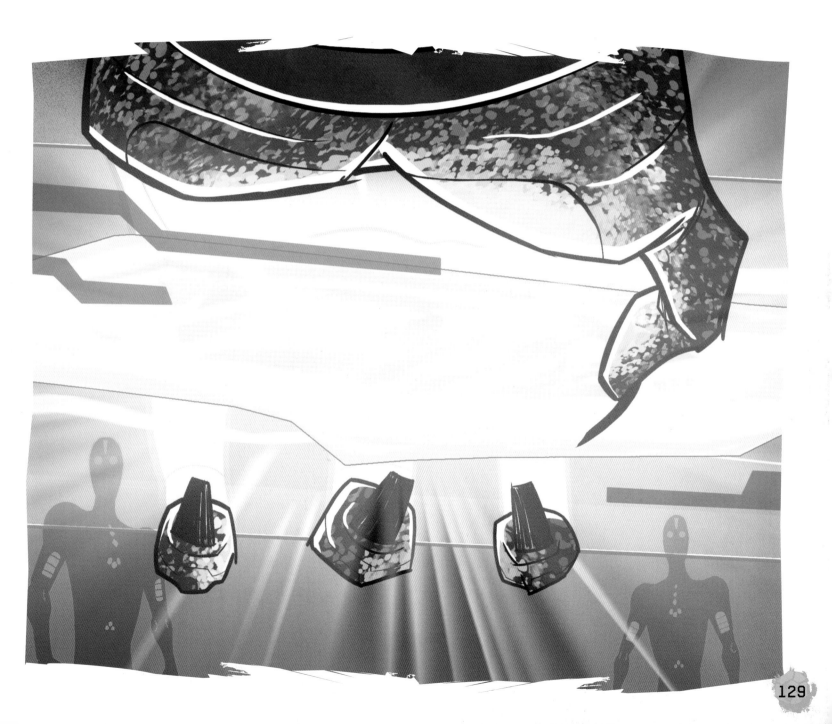

With an immense **ROAR** the creature jumped to its feet and, with a mighty arm, it swatted the Kraang-droids aside. They tumbled to the ground, sparking and smoking. The brain-like Kraang jumped from their broken robot bodies and slithered away.

The creature punched a hole in a wall and escaped....

Six months later, Leonardo, Raphael and Donatello were in the lair, watching TV, when Michelangelo came bounding into the room.

"Who wants to try my latest kitchen creation?" he asked. "We all love pizza. We all love milkshakes. So I combined them! I call it a P-shake!"

The other Turtles groaned ... nobody took him up on the offer!

Michelangelo took a big gulp and ... **BLEARGH!** He spat it out in disgust.

"Where did I go wrong?" he asked himself.

While Mikey poured away the remains of his P-shake, an item on the news grabbed the Turtles' attention. The newsreader began a story about New York's sewers.

"I'm Joan Grody with a sewer shocker!" the reporter said. "Were city sewer workers attacked ... by a giant monster?"

The Turtles didn't want the city's attention being drawn to the sewers – it would be very bad news for the secret lair.

"The last thing we want is some creature causing trouble in the sewers, or news crews down here looking for him," said Leonardo. "We've got to track this guy down and stop him ourselves."

"There's a tunnel number in the background of the news report," said Donatello. "Tunnel 281."

"Let's go!" said Leonardo.

The Turtles quickly found Tunnel 281, but the only signs of any strange creature were a few large footprints.

"What the heck made these footprints?" asked Leonardo.

"Feet," said Michelangelo, crouching to examine them. "Really big feet."

Suddenly, the noise of a huge battle tore through the tunnel and the Turtles charged towards the sounds to investigate.

They rounded a corner and saw a giant mutant alligator battling a group of Kraang-droids. The alligator grabbed two droids as if they were tiny dolls and smashed them together. With a powerful swipe of its tail, it sent another Kraang-droid flying into a wall. A pink Kraang brain-thing scurried out of the broken robot.

"Awesome!" Raphael said.

"Wow, I never thought I'd feel sorry for the Kraang." whispered Donatello.

Just as the Kraang-droids were on the
brink of defeat, one of them fired a massive
blaster cannon at the raging creature.

The blast hit the creature in the chest
and it collapsed to the ground.

The remaining Kraang-droids surrounded the injured mutant.

"Tell Kraang in what place can be found the power cell!" demanded one of the droids.

"NEVER!" screamed the creature.

"Then Kraang will continue to inflict pain," said another Kraang-droid.

"We've got to help him," Mikey whispered.

Mikey was about to leap in to save the creature, but Leo grabbed him.

"Mikey, we don't know anything about this guy," said Leonardo. "He could be even more dangerous than the Kraang."

"But that 'gator dude needs our help!" Mikey replied, "I can't wait around for you cowards!"

Michelangelo couldn't stand by while the creature was being hurt. He shrugged off Leo's hand and sprang into battle.

CRACK! He knocked one Kraang-droid out with a blow from his nunchucks and a flying kick toppled another.

Back at the lair, the Turtles began to argue about what to do with the creature. Donatello wanted to chain him up, but Michelangelo said that would be wrong.

"What's all the commotion?" asked Splinter as he entered the room.

"Mikey brought home a dangerous monster just because it was hurt!" said Raphael.

"There is no monster more dangerous than a lack of compassion," responded Splinter.

The Turtles told Splinter about the creature's fight and the power cell the Kraang wanted.

"You made a wise decision, Michelangelo," said Splinter. The Turtles were shocked to hear this. "I can't believe I just said that, either," Splinter continued.

But, to be cautious, he told Michelangelo to chain the creature until they knew more about him. "We need to learn what he knows about the Kraang."

Donatello, Raphael and Leonardo returned to Tunnel 281 to look for the missing power cell, while Michelangelo stayed in the lair.

When the giant alligator woke up he was furious to be in chains.

"SET ME FREE!" he roared.

"My brothers and I saved you from the Kraang," Mikey said calmly. "We brought you home with us so you could get better. Would you like some of my famous pizza-noodle soup?" Mikey offered him a steaming bowl.

"This is the best thing I have ever tasted!" said the creature.

"All right!" said Michelangelo. "Somebody finally likes my cooking!"

The creature and Michelangelo became friends. Mikey undid the chains and gave him a name: Leatherhead.

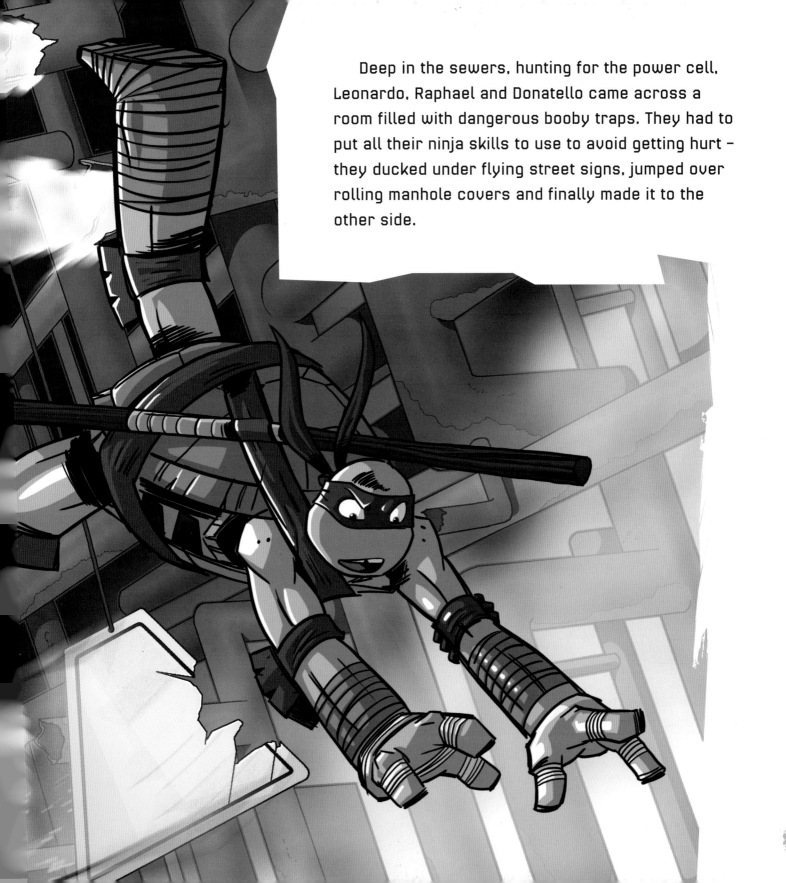

Deep in the sewers, hunting for the power cell,
Leonardo, Raphael and Donatello came across a
room filled with dangerous booby traps. They had to
put all their ninja skills to use to avoid getting hurt –
they ducked under flying street signs, jumped over
rolling manhole covers and finally made it to the
other side.

The Turtles found the power cell in the next room and took it back to the lair.

They couldn't believe Michelangelo had unchained the giant alligator.

"What if he goes berserk?" Leonardo asked.

"Don't worry," Michelangelo replied. "Leatherhead is totally mellow."

While his brothers discussed Leatherhead, Donatello inspected the power cell.

"It could power anything – a torch, a blaster cannon, even a Kraang spaceship!"

As soon as Donnie mentioned the Kraang, Leatherhead exploded with rage. **"KRAANG!"** he roared. Then, when Leatherhead saw the power cell, he grew even angrier.

"THIEVES!" he growled, and lashed out at the Turtles, fighting to get the power cell back.

"Stop!" Splinter commanded, stepping directly into Leatherhead's path. "Get away from my sons!"

Leatherhead lunged for Splinter, but Splinter was too fast for him. The giant mutant stopped fighting, snatched the power cell and ran away.

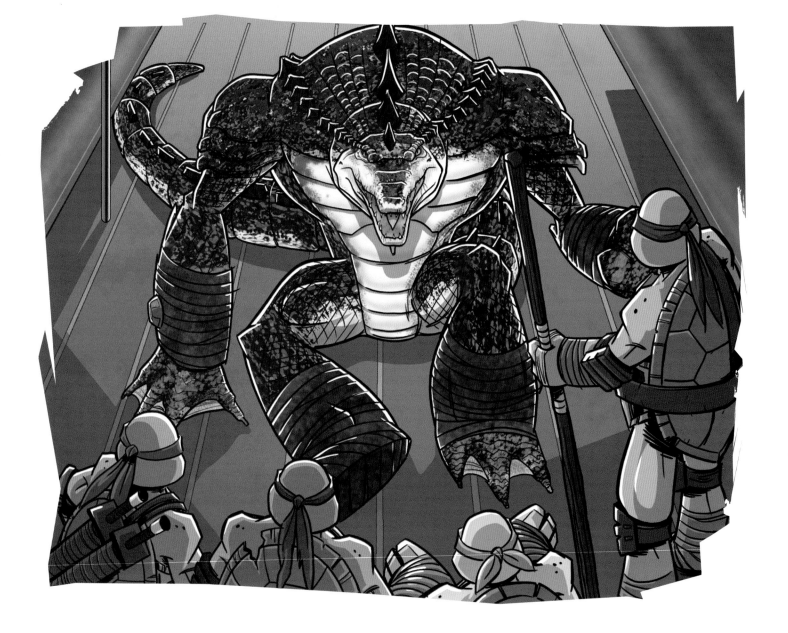

The Turtles chased Leatherhead until they reached an old subway carriage in an abandoned station. This was Leatherhead's home.

"Dude!" Michelangelo said sternly as he entered the carriage. "Friends don't beat up friends!"

"I'm sorry," said Leatherhead. "There are forces in me I can't always control."

The Turtles gathered in the carriage and Leatherhead began his story.

"The Kraang found me as a young 'gator," he said. "They took me to their dimension, mutated me, and tried to turn me into a living weapon."

Leatherhead continued. "This cell is very important – it powers the Kraang's portal to Earth. I stole it and escaped so that other Kraang couldn't enter this dimension. They would do anything to get it back...."

Suddenly, a blast rocked the train carriage. An army of Kraang-droids had tracked them down!

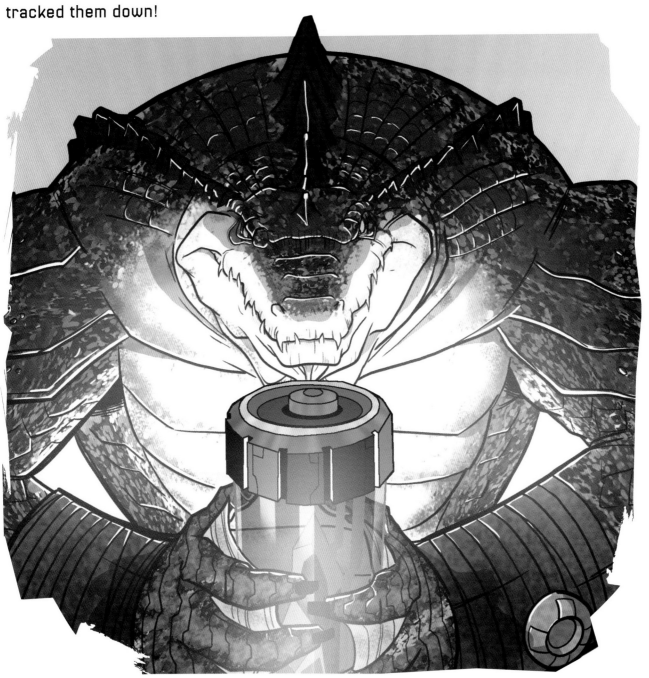

"GIVE TO KRAANG THE POWER CELL!" a robot voice ordered.

"Donnie, can you get this subway carriage running?" asked Leonardo.

But Donatello knew that, without electricity, there was no way he could get the rusty old train moving.

Leatherhead handed the power cell to Donatello. "You have trusted me," said Leatherhead. "Now I am trusting you."

With that, he hopped out of the train door to fight the Kraang.

Michelangelo, Leonardo and Raphael fought off the Kraang as they smashed through the carriage windows.

Meanwhile, Donatello connected the power cell to the train's engine. "I think I got it!" he exclaimed.

The last wire sparked and crackled as it touched the cell.

The train blasted away from the Kraang, leaving Leatherhead to fight alone.
It shot through the tunnel, going faster and faster banging and clanging along the
twisting rails. Sparks flew from the wheels as Donatello unhooked the power cell
and tried to apply the brakes.

The carriage finally screeched to a stop. The Turtles were safe for now, but they were worried.

Would Leatherhead survive another battle with the Kraang? And would the Kraang come looking for the Turtles to recover their power cell?

Only one thing was certain – the battle with the Kraang would continue another day....

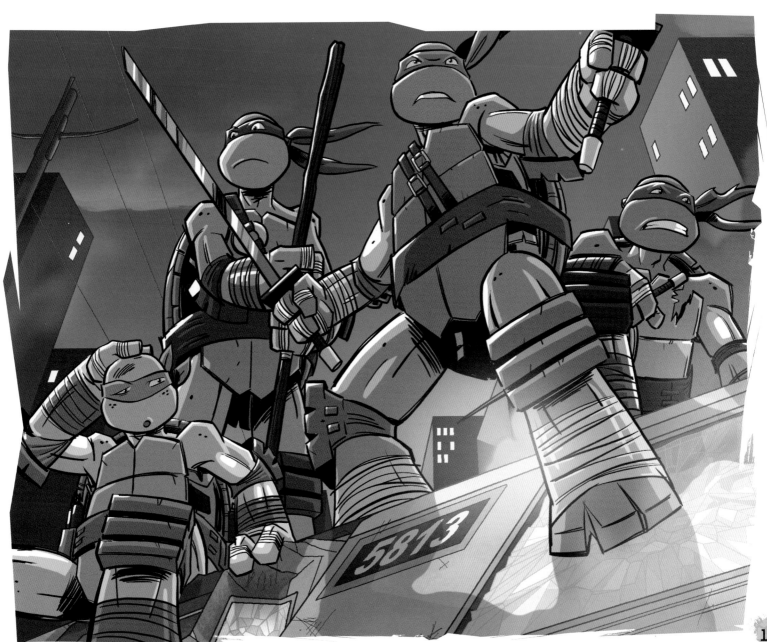